BATGIRL

DC SUPER HEROES

AN ORIGIN STORY

raintree
a Capstone company — publishers for children

Raintree is an imprint of Capstone Global Library Limited, a company
incorporated in England and Wales having its registered office at 264
Banbury Road, Oxford, OX2 7DY – Registered company number: 6695582

www.raintree.co.uk
myorders@raintree.co.uk

Designed by Hilary Wacholz
Contributing artists: Luciano Vecchio, Dan Schoenin, Erik Doescher,
Mike DeCarlo, Lee Loughridge and Leonel Castellani
Printed and bound in India

978 1 3982 0600 7 (hardback)
978 1 3982 0601 4 (paperback)

British Library Cataloguing in Publication Data
A full catalogue record for this book is available from the British Library.

BATGIRL

AN ORIGIN STORY

WRITTEN BY
LAURIE S. SUTTON

ILLUSTRATED BY
DARIO BRIZUELA

BATMAN CREATED BY
BOB KANE WITH BILL FINGER

Barbara Gordon spends a quiet night at home with her father. His name is James Gordon. He is the Police **commissioner** of Gotham City. That means he is the boss of all the police in the city.

4

Suddenly there is a loud knock at the front door. It's Gil Mason. He is second-in-command to Commissioner Gordon. He has two cops with him.

"I'm sorry, Commissioner, but you're under arrest," Mason says. The cops put handcuffs on Barbara's father.

"This has to be a mistake!" Barbara says. "Dad hasn't done anything wrong."

"He's charged with taking **bribes** from a crime boss named Rupert Thorne," Mason says. "That's against the law."

Barbara's father is taken away.

The next night, Batman comes
to visit Barbara. He is her father's
friend.

"I believe your father is innocent," Batman says.

"Batman, there's going to be a **rally** for my dad," Barbara says. "Will you come? People should know you're on his side?"

"No," Batman says. "I have to look for **proof** to clear your father instead."

Batman leaves to start his search.

"I have to think of a way for Batman to show up at the rally, one way or another," Barbara decides.

A large crowd gathers in the city centre. People have come to show their support for Commissioner Gordon. Gil Mason is on stage giving a speech. A figure in a Bat-costume stands on a nearby rooftop.

GOTHAM CITY RALLY

"Look! It's Batman!" someone shouts. "I knew he would come!" Everyone cheers.

No one in the crowd knows it's really Barbara Gordon! She is dressed like Batman.

Suddenly a car speeds down the middle of the road. It's going to hit the stage! Barbara thinks fast. She pulls down a rally banner. It falls on the speeding car. The driver can't see. He swerves and crashes.

A masked man gets out of the
front of the car. He tries to run away.
Barbara chases him. She throws a
rubbish bin lid like a Batarang. The
bad guy gets knocked down.

Barbara and some police officers catch him. The criminal is a **coward**. He starts to confess everything.

"Everything was a set up!" the thug says. "The attack was supposed to make Gil Mason look good. He wants to take over as police commissioner. He **framed** Gordon to get him out of the way."

At that moment, Batman arrives like a shadow in the night.

"I have proof," Batman says. "I've been doing **undercover** detective work to get the same information."

Batman puts Bat-cuffs on the bad guy. He turns to face Barbara in her Batsuit.

"I don't know who you are, but you did great work," Batman says. "It seems there's a new member of the 'Batman Family' in Gotham City. Welcome to the family, Batgirl!"

From that day on, Batman becomes Batgirl's teacher. He helps sharpen her crime-fighting skills. He teaches martial arts like judo and karate.

Batgirl is a talented and athletic gymnast. She can leap and tumble and swing on a Batrope. Her skills give her an extra edge.

Batgirl is a genius with computers. She uses them to gather information on criminals. The **data** helps solve crimes. She can use Batman's super Batcomputer better than he can!

Inspired by Batman's Utility Belt, Batgirl creates one for herself. It holds many tools for catching crooks. It has Batarangs, smoke pellets, nets and a Batrope.

Batgirl rides a motorbike called the Batcycle. She uses it to patrol Gotham City and help Batman defeat super-villains.

Batgirl faces many of Batman's foes.

The Joker is a crazy criminal. He dresses like the joker on a playing card. His laugh is like a hyena.

Clayface looks like a man made of mud. He can shape-shift into any form. He can become an elephant or turn to ooze.

Catwoman is a clever cat burglar. She loves stealing valuables that have something to do with cats or animals. Even though Catwoman is a thief, she helps Batgirl sometimes.

Batgirl sometime teams up with her friend, Supergirl, to battle the terrible twosome: Poison Ivy and Harley Quinn. But even Ivy's plant-growing powers and Harley's crazy **antics** are no match for the super heroes.

Tonight, super-villain Livewire is on the loose. She became a being of living electricity after getting struck by lightning.

Livewire has been in prison. But when she escapes, the first thing she does is cause trouble for Gotham City.

31

Livewire is weak after using her powers to escape jail. She gets strong by sucking up electricity.

The city's main power plant feeds her. Soon all the electrical power goes out in Gotham City. Batgirl goes to the power plant to stop Livewire.

"I'm not shocked to see it's you causing all this trouble, Livewire," Batgirl says.

"Ha! I'm just getting started!"
Livewire replies. She throws a
bolt of electricity at Batgirl.

Batgirl uses her gymnastic skills to flip out of the way. She lands next to an emergency fire hose.

Once she sees the hose, Batgirl knows she has a way to defeat the super-villain.

Batgirl reaches into her Utility Belt for a Batarang. She throws the Batarang at Livewire.

FIRE HOSE

The villain blasts the Batarang with more electricity.

"Ha, ha! That won't stop me!" Livewire says gleefully. "And neither will you!"

Livewire is too busy laughing at her **foe** to notice Batgirl is aiming the fire hose at her.

Suddenly, a strong gush of water hits the villain! Water and electricity do not mix. The villain shorts out!

FIRE HOSE

Batgirl ties Livewire up with the hose. The police come to take Livewire back to prison.

Commissioner Gordon is with them. "Thank you for catching Livewire, Batgirl," Gordon says. "You saved Gotham City."

He doesn't know that Batgirl is his daughter, Barbara. Someday she will tell him. But for now, it's part of being a caped crusader.

BATGIRL ™

REAL NAME: BARBARA GORDON

ROLE: CRIME FIGHTER

BASE: GOTHAM CITY

Barbara is the daughter of Gotham City's police commissioner, James Gordon. She made her own Batsuit and fights crime without her father's knowledge. She has many special skills that help her to protect the city.

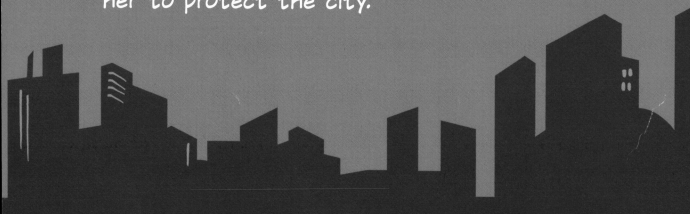

THE AUTHOR

LAURIE S. SUTTON is a comic book writer and editor. She is also the author of *The Mystery of the Aztec Tomb* and *The Secret of the Sea Creature* from the You Choose Stories: Scooby-Doo series. She currently resides in Florida, USA.

THE ILLUSTRATOR

DARIO BRIZUELA was born in Buenos Aires, Argentina, and as a teen he began studying in an art school – doing drawing, sculpture, painting and more. After discovering super hero comic books, his goal was draw his favourite characters. He has worked for major publishers like Dark Horse Comics, IDW, Viz Media, DC Comics, and Marvel Comics. He has also worked for Hasbro and LEGO. Star Wars Tales, Super Friends, Justice League Unlimited and Scooby-Doo are just a few of his artistic contributions.

GLOSSARY

antics playful or funny acts or actions

bribe money or gifts used to persuade someone to do something; especially something illegal or dishonest

commissioner an official who heads up the administration of a government department

coward someone who acts without bravery

data information or facts

foe an enemy

proof facts or evidence that show something is true

rally a large gathering of people who come together to take action

undercover done in secret, especially in spying activities

DISCUSSION QUESTIONS

Write down your answers. Refer back to the story for help.

QUESTION 1.

Why does Barbara think it's important that people know Batman is on her father's side? Look at the picture and draw conclusions using what you see.

QUESTION 2.

Why do you think Gil Mason wanted to be the commissioner?

QUESTION 3.

In this image, Barbara is fighting Harley Quinn. Look at what she is doing. What skills does she need to be a good crime fighter?

QUESTION 4.

Who is your favourite villain? Why?

READ THEM ALL!!

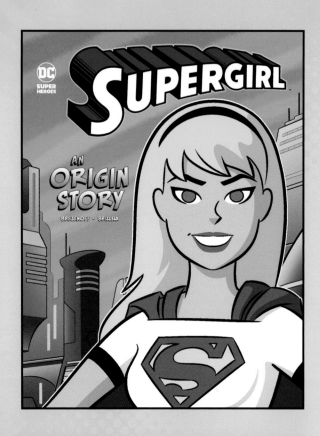

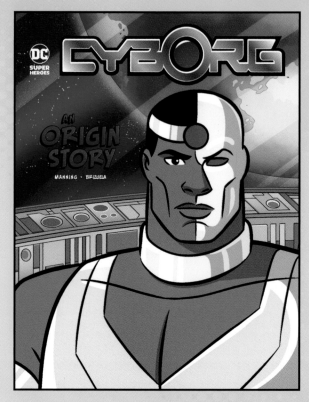

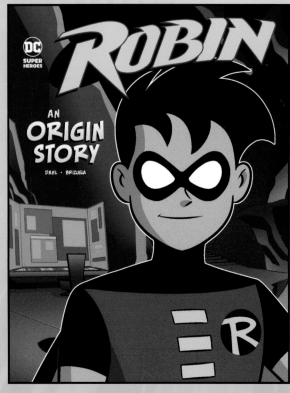

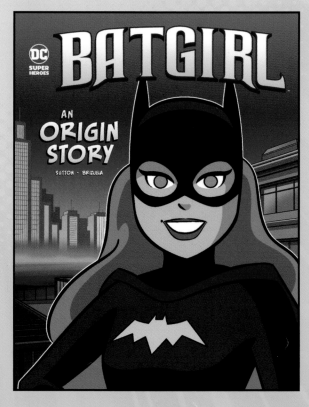